William's
WORKSHOP

a one-act play
in
five scenes

by
Susan Gates

William spends lots of time in
his mysterious workshop.
Is he inventing marvellous things,
as he tells his friend Emily?
Or are Danny and Laura right when
they call him "a great big liar"?

Characters:

WILLIAM – a small, shy, day-dreaming boy

EMILY – William's friend

2

THE AVENGER – a huge, fearsome robot

WILLIAM'S MUM – only her voice is heard

LAURA AND DANNY – two bullies who make fun of William's daydreams

3

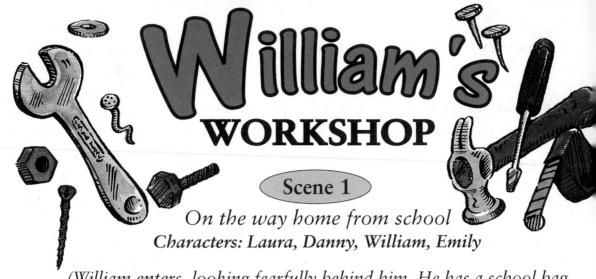

William's WORKSHOP

Scene 1

On the way home from school
Characters: Laura, Danny, William, Emily

(William enters, looking fearfully behind him. He has a school bag on his back. He is followed by Danny and Laura.)

LAURA: Wimpy William! Wimpy William!

DANNY: He'll run away in a minute. Just watch him. Why don't you run away, wimp?

WILLIAM: I won't run away.

LAURA: Oh! He's being brave today. Go on, tell us about your workshop again, William. Tell us what you make in there.

DANNY: (*Sarcastically*) Didn't you know? William makes incredible things in there. He makes computers that talk to you and do your homework. And robot dogs that bark and fetch your slippers. He makes all sorts of wonderful stuff in there. He's a brilliant genius, an inventor. At least, that's what he's always telling us.

LAURA: (*Sarcastically*) Oh, I didn't know that. I didn't know he was a genius. I thought he was a little wimpy baby who can't fight, who runs away. I thought he was a daydreamer, like teacher says.

4

DANNY: And I thought he was a great big liar – who says he's inventing things in his workshop when he isn't.

WILLIAM: It's true, it's true. I do invent things. But they don't always work. I mean, I never said they worked, did I?

LAURA: He's making excuses now!

WILLIAM: I'm not, I'm just…

DANNY: (*Interrupting*) Well, I think it's about time we saw one of these wonderful inventions. Go on, William, bring in your latest invention. Bring it to school tomorrow.

WILLIAM: Well, I would do. Honest I would. But my latest invention is really big. It's too big to bring into school. And anyway, it's not finished yet.

LAURA: More excuses! He's just trying to wriggle out of it!

DANNY: So what is this big invention then, William? Is it a space rocket or something? A rocket that'll fly you to Mars?

WILLIAM: (*Quietly*) Don't be silly. I couldn't make one of those in my workshop.

DANNY: (*Not listening*) Because if it's a space rocket you could fly it to school, William. Fly it to school and land on the football field!

LAURA: Anyway, your workshop's not even a proper workshop. It's just a crumbly old garden shed!

WILLIAM: (*Ignoring their taunts, with a far-away, dreamy look on his face*) I'd like to fly to Mars though. It'd be really brilliant. It's beautiful on Mars. It's called the Red Planet and there are deserts there and high mountains, even volcanoes…

DANNY: Oh no, off he goes, daydreaming again.

LAURA: He's hopeless, isn't he?

(*Danny and Laura dance around William, jeering. Laura pulls his bag off his back.*)

WILLIAM: (*Trying to catch the bag as they throw it to one another*) Leave my bag alone. I've got secret plans in there. Plans for my latest invention.

(*Laura laughs and throws his bag away.*)

DANNY: I'll tell you what William is. He's a coward who won't take a dare.

WILLIAM: I *will* take dares. I will.

LAURA: (*Looking around*) OK then, jump off this high wall. Look, it's easy. (*Jumping off*) Wheee!

DANNY: See, it's easy-peasy. (*Climbing up.*) Anyone can do it. Little kids can do it. I'm Superman!

(*Danny leaps off the wall, arms outspread. William climbs up, looks down, hesitates, his knees trembling.*)

LAURA: Oh no, he's scared of heights, he's scared of *everything*.

WILLIAM: I'm not, I'm not. I can do it. Just give me time. Don't rush me.

LAURA: Well, we're not waiting here all day. We're going home for tea!

DANNY: And tomorrow, you make sure you bring your latest invention. You bring it to school. Or else!

(They run off laughing. Distant cries of 'Wimpy William! Wimpy William!' are heard.)

(Emily enters. She picks up William's school bag. Then she looks up and sees William, on the wall.)

EMILY: William, what on earth are you doing up there? Have those two been following you home again? Have they been bullying you?

(William climbs down off the wall.)

WILLIAM: I'm hopeless, I am – hopeless. I don't know why you want me as a friend.

EMILY: Why are you hopeless?

WILLIAM: 'Cos I can't jump off high walls. I can't take a dare.

EMILY: Is that all? I can't jump off high walls either. I wouldn't *want* to jump off walls. You'll only break your neck or something. It's stupid, just forget about it. Look, here's your school bag.

WILLIAM: (*Grabs bag, opens it, checks inside*) Good, they're safe. They're very important. They're my secret plans. I can't lose them now because I've nearly finished. I've nearly finished my very best invention. It's…

EMILY: (*Interrupting*) Oh no. You haven't been going on about your workshop again? And about what you're inventing? It's no wonder they make fun of you, William, when you tell lies like that. After all, no one's seen a single one of these marvellous inventions yet.

WILLIAM: They're not lies, they're not lies! I *am* making things in there. I'm making…

EMILY: Look, you don't need to boast to me, William. I'm your friend, remember. Are you coming to Swimming Club tonight? Shall I come round to your house to call for you?

WILLIAM: I can't – I'll be busy in my workshop.

EMILY: (*Shrugging helplessly*) OK then. I'll see you at school tomorrow.

(*Exit Emily. William looks sadly after her.*)

WILLIAM: (*To himself*) Well, I suppose I'll just have to admit it. I don't invent anything in my workshop. Not things that'll work, anyhow. Oh, I build things all right. I'm always building things. But they never turn out like I see them in my mind. And they never work like I want them to. So I'm in real trouble now. What am I going to do? My latest invention doesn't work either. But they want to see it tomorrow. Or else!

(*William puts his school bag on his shoulder, gives a deep, hopeless sigh, then trudges miserably off stage.*)

Scene 2

Outside William's workshop
Characters: Danny, Laura

*(Danny and Laura are standing on tiptoe,
looking over a hedge into William's garden.)*

LAURA: See, I told you, it's not a workshop at all. It's just an old garden shed.

DANNY: Do you think he's in there?

LAURA: Bet he is. He's always in there. *(Rather longingly)* Dreaming wonderful dreams.

DANNY: *(In an accusing voice)* You're not sticking up for him, are you?

LAURA: *(Quickly)* No, of course not. Would I do something like that? Let's go in the garden, shall we? Let's go in and give him a fright!

DANNY: We'll creep around outside and we'll shout "Boo!"

LAURA: We'll scratch on the windows and moan like ghosts. Whooo!

DANNY: We'll get him. We'll scare him to death.

LAURA: Come on. There's a gap in this hedge.

(They wriggle through the gap, and creep forward.)

DANNY: Can you see anything? Why are the windows glowing like that? Look, they're all fiery red. What's he doing in there?

(There is a sound of metal being hammered.)

LAURA: And what's that noise? What's going on in there?

(A sudden deep roaring sound comes from the workshop. Danny and Laura jump with alarm, clutch each other in fear.)

DANNY: I've just remembered. I've got to get back home. I've got to – got to – go shopping with my Mum.

LAURA: Yes, I've got to go as well. We'll get him though, we'll get him tomorrow morning.

(They shove and push each other to get back through the gap in the hedge. They run off. The sound of roaring and hammering gets louder, then fades away.)

Scene 3

William's workshop

Characters: William, the Avenger, the voice of William's mum

*(The Avenger is sitting behind William. His head is lowered.
He is slumped in the chair. William is standing, with his back to the
Avenger. He has a control panel in his hand.)*

WILLIAM: (*To himself*) I wish Laura and Danny had been here just
now. Those bullies would never believe what happened!
(*To the Avenger.*) You're my best invention ever – my
robot. I'm going to call you the Avenger. I know you're
made out of bits of rubbish. I know you look a mess. But
you really work. Not like all my other inventions. You're
even better than I imagined! Go on! Lift your right hand.

WILLIAM: *(To the Avenger)* What's wrong? You did it just now. You roared like a lion. Like this: Gurrrr! I wish they'd heard you. And your eyes glowed like fire.

(William presses the control panel again. Nothing happens.)

WILLIAM: I bet no one will believe me now. They'll still think I'm telling lies about my inventions.

(Behind William, the Avenger's right hand twitches and lifts up, very slowly, with a clanking noise.)

WILLIAM: What was that? Who's there?

(The Avenger lifts his head and stares at him. William turns round.)

WILLIAM: *(Joyfully)* Oh Avenger, you're working. You're working. I knew you would! Look at those burning eyes!

(He rushes over to the Avenger, pressing buttons on the control panel.)

WILLIAM: Right, Avenger, show me how scary you are. Shake your fist. Go on, shake your fist!

(The Avenger gives a cheery wave.)

WILLIAM: No, no.

(William picks up a screwdriver. He uses it to tighten a screw in the Avenger's elbow.)

WILLIAM: Now shake your fist!

(The Avenger shakes his fist about and growls.)

AVENGER: Gurrrr!

WILLIAM: (*Proudly*) There, I knew you could roar like a lion. Go on, do it again, Avenger.

AVENGER: Miaow!

WILLIAM: Still a few minor adjustments to make.

(*He tightens a screw in the Avenger's neck.*)

WILLIAM: There – now roar like a lion!

(*The Avenger gets up from the chair with a great clanking of metal. He stomps about, waving his fist.*)

AVENGER: Gurrrr!

(The Avenger faces William, shakes his fist at him, threateningly. He roars fiercely at him.)

WILLIAM: No, no! You mustn't fight me. Or my friends. You only scare people I don't like. Only bullies like Laura and Danny. Understand?

(William presses buttons on the control panel. The Avenger unclenches his fist, waves clumsily at William.)

AVENGER: *(In a deep, menacing, robot voice)* Friends. Friends.

WILLIAM: *(Amazed)* You can talk! That's incredible! I didn't program you to do that. Go on, say something else.

(William presses the control panel. The Avenger's shoulders slump, his head droops. He drags himself back to the chair and slumps into it, motionless.)

WILLIAM: *(To himself)* He talked. He actually talked. And he obeyed my commands. I said, "Shake your fist," and he did!

17

(*William walks over to the Avenger, pressing the control panel.*)

WILLIAM: Come on, Avenger, do it again. Shake your fist! Walk about! Say something!

(*The Avenger does not move. William shrugs.*)

WILLIAM: Oh well, I expect you're just having a rest. But at least you really work. Talk and walk and do what I tell you. Now they'll all have to believe me. Even Danny and Laura.

WILLIAM'S MUM: (*From offstage*) William, it's teatime. Hurry up. It's ready NOW!

WILLIAM: I'd better go.

(*He turns to take one last look at the Avenger.*)

WILLIAM: It'll be brilliant. Because I'm taking you to school, Avenger. Just like they wanted me to. They'll wish they'd never made fun of me and my inventions. Now I've got you, Avenger, those bullies had better watch out!

WILLIAM'S MUM: (*Angrily, offstage*) William! Your tea's getting cold!

(*Exit William. The Avenger is still slumped in his seat. Then, very slowly, he raises his head. He stares menacingly at the audience and bares his teeth like a wolf.*)

AVENGER: Gurrrr!

Scene 4

On the way to school
Characters: William, Danny, Laura, the Avenger, Emily

*(William enters, his school bag on his shoulder, whistling casually.
The Avenger is hidden, crouched behind a wall.
Danny and Laura enter.)*

DANNY: There's William. Let's have some fun.

LAURA: (*Pulling him back*) Wait. Remember last night. Remember the horrible roaring noise from his workshop? And the fiery glow from the windows? And how we ran away?

DANNY: What fiery glow? I didn't see anything. And I didn't run away! You're imagining things.

(*Danny walks towards William.*)

DANNY: (*Pretending to look all around him*) Well, where is it, William? Where's this wonderful new invention?

LAURA: We told you to bring it to school today.

DANNY: Or else!

AVENGER: (*From his hiding place*) Gurrrr!

LAURA: What was that noise?

DANNY: I didn't hear anything.

LAURA: Come on, Danny. Let's leave him alone.

DANNY: (*Ignoring her*) So where is it, William? I can't see it.

WILLIAM: I've got it with me.

DANNY: Is it invisible? Bet that's what you're going to tell me, isn't it? Your latest experiment is invisible. And guess what, nobody can see it but you!

LAURA: Let's go, Danny. William's all right really. Let's just leave him alone.

DANNY: (*Ignoring her*) You don't invent anything, do you William? Except for great big lies. You're really good at inventing those.

AVENGER: (*From his hiding place*) Gurrrr!

LAURA: (*Looking round, shivering*) There's a big dog round here somewhere.

WILLIAM: (*Taking the control panel out of his backpack*) If I can't invent things, what's this then?

(*He presses buttons on the panel. The Avenger gets up from his hiding place. Clanking, roaring, shaking his fists, he lurches towards Danny and Laura. They run away, yelling in terror.*)

WILLIAM: (*Overjoyed*) Yes! Brilliant! You scared them away! That was great, Avenger. Did you see them run? And they called me a coward. They called me a wimp!

AVENGER: (*Growling softly*) Gurrrr!

EMILY: (*From offstage*) William!

WILLIAM: Someone's coming! Get back in your hiding place, Avenger.

(*William presses the control panel and the Avenger clanks away and hides. Emily enters.*)

WILLIAM: Phew! It's only you, Emily. I thought it was Danny and Laura coming back.

EMILY: Have they been teasing you again?

WILLIAM: (*Happily*) You must be joking. They'll never dare make fun of me again. Not ever. Not now I've got the Avenger!

EMILY: The Avenger? What are you talking about? Oh, William, this isn't another one of your stories, is it?

WILLIAM: See for yourself. See if I'm telling stories or not!

(*William presses buttons on the control panel. The Avenger comes out of his hiding place.*)

EMILY: (*Terrified*) Run, William, run!

(*She tries to drag him away.*)

WILLIAM: (*Laughing*) It's OK, Emily. Don't be scared. He won't hurt you. I can control him. He does exactly what I say. Just watch this!

(*William gives a demonstration. He presses the control panel and gives the Avenger orders.*)

WILLIAM: Stand on one leg, Avenger!

(*The Avenger does so, clumsily.*)

WILLIAM: Right! That's enough! Now, rub your stomach, Avenger.

(*The Avenger obeys but begins to growl softly in protest.*)

WILLIAM: Now rub your head at the same time!

(*The Avenger obeys, clumsily.*)

WILLIAM: I, William, am your Master. You must obey my every command!

EMILY: (*Very impressed*) Wow! That's incredible, William. And you invented him in your workshop?

(*William nods proudly. The Avenger is still rubbing his head and stomach. William presses buttons.*)

WILLIAM: Stop doing that now.

AVENGER: (*Stopping*) Gurrrr!

EMILY: I'm sorry I didn't believe you, William. About all those things you said you invented. I'm really sorry. I should never have said you were telling stories.

WILLIAM: (*Embarrassed*) That's OK. Just forget it.

AVENGER: (*Loudly*) Gurrrr!

EMILY: Why is he growling like that? Why are his eyes lighting up? They're like red fires. They're staring straight at me!

WILLIAM: I don't know. I didn't tell him to do that.

(*He fiddles with the control panel. The Avenger takes a step towards Emily, raises his arm, shakes his fist.*)

EMILY: William, he's coming to get me. Make him stop!

WILLIAM: (*Frantically pressing the control panel*) No, Avenger, no. She's a friend, a friend. Remember, I taught you that word. We don't hurt our friends. I told you! I am your Master!

AVENGER: (*In a roaring, menacing, robot voice*) I am the Mighty Avenger. No one is my Master!

(*He beats his metal chest, roars, take another clanking step towards Emily.*)

EMILY: Help, help!

(*She runs away. The Avenger pursues her.*)

WILLIAM: (*Shouting after him*) Look what you've done now! You've frightened Emily. I didn't program you to scare my friends!

(*There is a faint roaring in the distance. William is left on the stage, still uselessly pressing the control panel. He looks lonely and bewildered.*)

WILLIAM: (*To himself*) He wasn't supposed to do that. He wasn't supposed to scare away my friend!

(*William exits, running. We hear him shouting.*)

WILLIAM: Come back, Avenger, come back! Leave my friend alone!

On the way to school
Characters: William, the Avenger, Emily

(The Avenger strides on to the stage.
He boasts to the audience.)

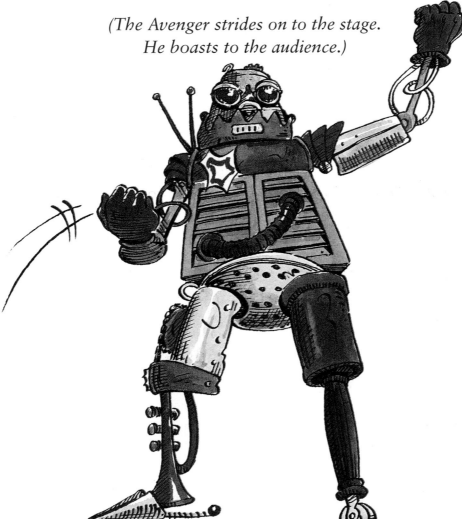

AVENGER: I am the Mighty Avenger! I rule the world.
People tremble when they hear my name!

(He roars and beats his metal chest. William rushes in.)

WILLIAM: There you are! Where's Emily? Where is she? You'd better not have hurt her! She's my friend. I told you, you're not supposed to scare my friends.

(*The Avenger turns towards William, menacingly. He takes a step forwards.*)

AVENGER: (*Boasting*) Friends? Friends? I have no friends. Everybody's scared of ME! Even you are scared of ME!

WILLIAM: (*Looking scared*) No, I'm not. I made you. I control you. You must obey me.

(*William presses buttons on the control panel.*)

WILLIAM: Move away!

(*The Avenger moves towards him and raises his arm.*)

WILLIAM: Put your arm down!

(*The Avenger raises his arm higher, shakes his fist at William.*)

AVENGER: Gurrrr!

WILLIAM: (*Frantically pressing buttons*) Switch off! Switch off!

(*The Avenger laughs, a deep, sinister laugh.*)

WILLIAM: What can I do now? This control panel is useless!

(*He throws the control panel away. The Avenger takes another step towards him. William looks round desperately. Suddenly he sees the high wall behind them. He has a brilliant idea.*)

WILLIAM: (*To the Avenger*) Bet you can't jump off that high wall.

(*The Avenger stops in mid-stride and turns to look at the wall.*)

AVENGER: That tiny little wall? Of course I can! I am the Mighty Avenger!

(*The Avenger beats his metal chest.*)

WILLIAM: Bet you can't. You're a wimp!

AVENGER: I'm not! I'm not! I am – AVENGER!

(*He roars, horribly.*)

WILLIAM: Go on, then, if you're so tough.
I dare you. I dare you to
jump off that wall.

AVENGER: Easy-peasy!

*(The Avenger climbs on to the wall.
He stands on the top, boasting.)*

AVENGER: I am Avenger. I take every dare.
No one can beat me.
I rule the world!

(*He jumps. As he lands there is a terrific noise of clashing metal. The Avenger lies on the floor in a tangled heap. He doesn't move. William approaches, very cautiously.*)

WILLIAM: Avenger? Avenger?

(*William lifts the Avenger's arm. The arm flops back. He lifts the other arm. The same thing happens.*)

WILLIAM: (*In an expressionless voice*) He's broken. He's wrecked.

AVENGER: (*Lifting his head slightly and whispering*) Friend.

(*The Avenger's head drops down again. William kneels beside him.*)

WILLIAM: What did you say, Avenger? Did you say something?

(*But the Avenger doesn't speak or move again.*
Emily creeps on to the stage. She taps William on the back.
William leaps up, startled.)

WILLIAM: Oh, it's you Emily! It's OK. He won't frighten you anymore. He's just a heap of scrap metal now. Look, his eyes don't glow anymore. The lights have gone out.

EMILY: (*Doubtfully*) You could mend him again. You could mend him in your workshop, if you wanted to.

WILLIAM: (*Thoughtfully*) I might be able to. But I don't think I want to. I don't like him. He scares me. He gets out of control.

(*William gazes at the Avenger.*)

EMILY: (*Trying to cheer him up*) Why don't you come swimming tonight, William? I'll call for you after tea.

WILLIAM: All right then. But I'm not giving up my inventions. I'll probably think of another one soon.

EMILY: Just don't make any more Avengers!

(*William takes one last look at the Avenger.*
Then he walks off with Emily, leaving the wreck of the Avenger behind him.
From off-stage we hear William's voice.)

WILLIAM: Actually, I've been thinking a lot about space ships lately. Did you know that there are volcanoes on Mars?

THE END